HEDGEHOG HAVEN

A Story of a
British Hedgerow Community

by Deborah Dennard

Illustrated by Robert Hynes

On the birth of Austin Parker Schmidt—D.D.

To all art teachers—R.H.

Book layout: Marcin D. Pilchowski
Editor: Judy Gitenstein
Editorial assistance: Chelsea Shriver

First edition 2001
10 9 8 7 6 5 4 3 2 1
Printed in China

Acknowledgments:
   Our very special thanks to Louis A. (Trooper) Walsh III of the Department of Herpetology at the Smithsonian Institution's National Zoological Park for his curatorial review.

Library of Congress Cataloging-in-Publication Data

Dennard, Deborah.
   Hedgehog haven : a story of a British hedgerow community / by Deborah Dennard; illustrated by Robert Hynes.—1st ed.
        p. cm.
     Summary: Follows a day in the life of a six-month-old hedgehog, who avoids the dangers of tractor, draft horse and fox, and feasts on insects and other treats in her British hedgerow community.
   ISBN 1-56899-987-9 (alk. paper) — ISBN 1-56899-988-7 (pbk. : alk. paper)
1. Hedgehogs—Juvenile fiction. [1. Hedgehogs—Fiction. 2. Hedgerow ecology—Fiction. 3. Country life—England—Fiction. 4. Ecology—Fiction.] I. Hynes, Robert, ill. II. Title.

PZ10.3.D386 He 2001
[E]—dc21

00-063741

HEDGEHOG HAVEN

A Story of a
British Hedgerow Community

by Deborah Dennard
Illustrated by Robert Hynes

Soundprints
Where Children Discover...

The sweet, spicy scent of heather tickles the nose of a hedgehog as she curls in her grassy day nest at the base of the hedgerow in southwestern England. She is sheltered in the shade of the double row of ancient hawthorn trees tangled in a great green web with smaller holly, oak, and elder trees.

The man-made row of plants stretches down the edges of the fields and pastures as far as the eye can see, turning the landscape into neat, green boxes and squares. Curled in a ball with her sharp spines sticking out in all directions like a tiny shield of needles, she is safe from danger—for now.

A whirring sound gets louder and louder as a tractor gets closer. The hedgehog curls into a tighter ball as the sharp blades of the mower narrowly miss her. The tractor continues on, mowing the tall grasses of the field.

The hedgehog is not aware of her narrow escape. She knows only that her day nap has been disturbed. Just six months old, she is young and less than cautious. Hungry, she scurries on her short, stubby legs through the freshly mown grass, snapping up spiders, beetles and grasshoppers as she goes. European goldfinches chirp their songs as they flit gracefully from thistle to thistle, feeding on the tiny seeds, but the hedgehog does not notice.

Nearby, a rabbit breaks away from the cover of the hedgerow, hopping at full speed. Only seconds behind is a swift, graceful fox. The hedgehog freezes as the unlucky rabbit satisfies the fox's hunger.

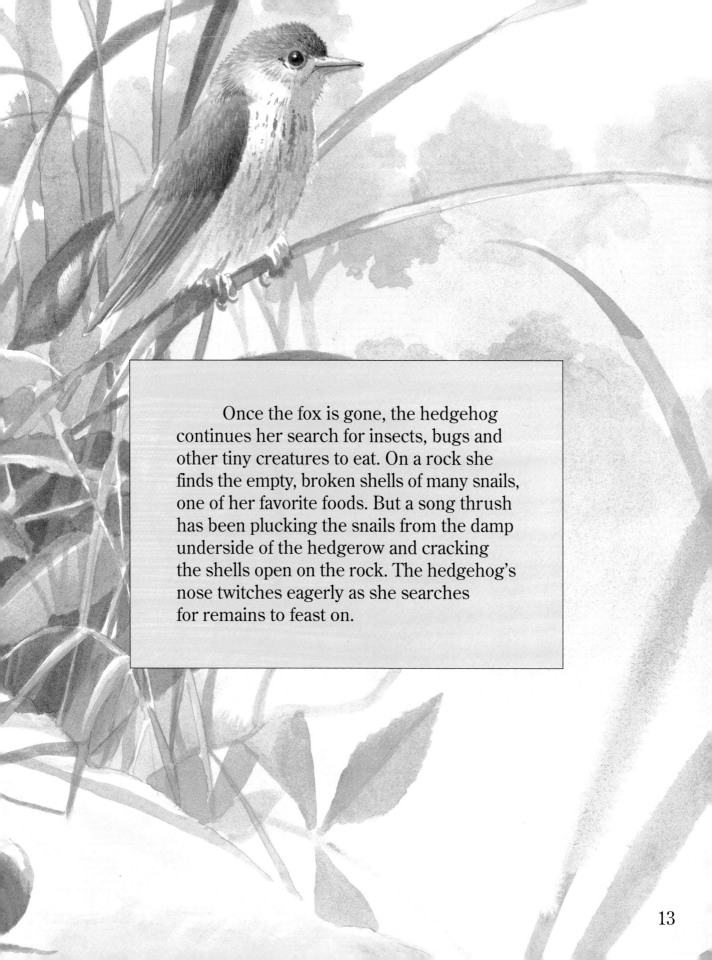

Once the fox is gone, the hedgehog
continues her search for insects, bugs and
other tiny creatures to eat. On a rock she
finds the empty, broken shells of many snails,
one of her favorite foods. But a song thrush
has been plucking the snails from the damp
underside of the hedgerow and cracking
the shells open on the rock. The hedgehog's
nose twitches eagerly as she searches
for remains to feast on.

She follows no path, but zigzags across the field framed by the hedgerows. The freshly mown grass provides plenty of food, from centipedes, to slugs, to woodlice and caterpillars. The hedgehog even tears into an ant bed to lap up the tasty ant eggs. As she feeds, she grunts and snorts and makes little belching noises.

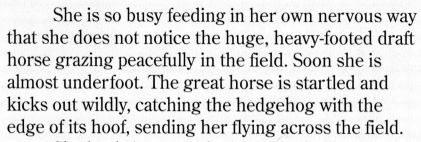

She is so busy feeding in her own nervous way that she does not notice the huge, heavy-footed draft horse grazing peacefully in the field. Soon she is almost underfoot. The great horse is startled and kicks out wildly, catching the hedgehog with the edge of its hoof, sending her flying across the field.

She lands in a soft clump of bluebells and primroses. Luckily, the kick has done no damage. Panting heavily, her heart beating even more quickly than usual, the hedgehog settles down to wait for the safety of the night. When she is older she will learn to wait for the darkness to begin her search for food.

The moon rises in a cloudless sky. A barn owl hoots then flies across the field. It lands near the top of the hedgerow over the hedgehog, knocking a nest of house sparrow eggs to the ground. The mother sparrow squawks and flies away. Underneath, the hedgehog hungrily laps up the broken eggs.

The hedghog is thirsty and heads for the gurgling stream on the opposite side of the field. Once there she finds far more than water.

A fisherman has left behind three fish heads from his day's catch. The hedgehog cannot resist the strong smell. She rolls in the fishy mess. The strong odor makes her own saliva froth and flow freely. Using her tongue and front feet, she spreads the saliva on her shoulders, head and tummy.

Fully anointed, she moves to the pebbly edge of the stream to drink. The rocks are slippery. She tumbles into the cool water. Paddling frantically with all four legs, she swims to the other side of the stream and pulls herself up on the shallow gravel edge.

This field has not yet been mown and the grass is tall and wild. The hedgehog waddles through the jungle of grass and bumps into another hedgehog! He is a young male, also on his own. Both hedgehogs are surprised and confused at their meeting. They snort and grunt as they sniff each other curiously. After a while they go their own ways. If they meet again when they are older, they may well have baby hedgehogs of their own.

Before the faintest trace of morning light begins to show on the eastern horizon, the hedgehog sets out for the hedgerow on the opposite side of the field. She nibbles on wild berries for their sweetness and the tiny insects that live inside.

As the sun begins to rise, the hedgehog pulls grasses around her in a cozy nest. Soon her nose is buried in the soft fur of her tummy. Her sharp spines stand at attention. Once again she is asleep and safe in the sheltering arms of the great ancient hedgerow.

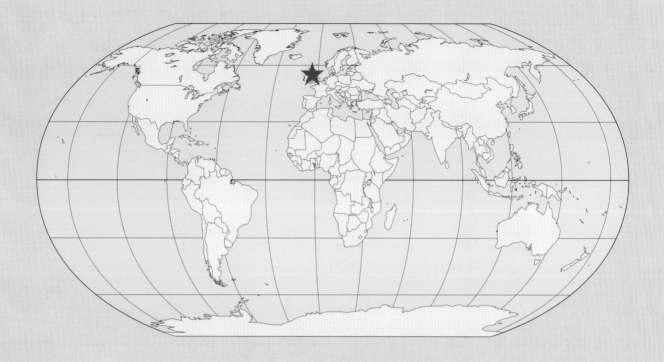

Hedgerow Communities, Great Britain

Great Britain is an island off the west coast of Europe and is about 89,000 square miles large, about the size of the state of Oregon. The countries of England, Scotland and Wales are all a part of Great Britain. People have occupied Britain for so many years there is very little wilderness left. Still, there are places for animals to live, places like hedgerow communities.

Hedgerow communities are man-made habitats designed to help farmers divide their property, fields and livestock. Since as early as the 12th century, miles and miles of tree fences called hedgerows have been planted and tended dividing the British landscape into a beautiful green patchwork. Hedgerows define the look of rural Britain. At the same time, they are home to many wild animals such as hedgehogs.

About Hedgerows and Hedgehogs

Hedgerows may be very old, with some of their oldest trees easily two hundred years old or more. Hedgerows are usually based on a double row of hawthorn trees planted two feet apart. Smaller elder, holly and oak trees grow in between with plants such as chickweed, grasses, bluebells, primroses, thistle and dandelions surrounding them. The plants grow together like a dense, living wall.

Half of Britain's mammals and many of its birds find their homes in hedgerows. Small birds that eat insects, seeds or fruits find plenty of food and excellent nesting spots in hedgerows. Mammals from foxes to badgers to weasels, moles and rabbits find food and shelter in hedgerows. Perhaps the most famous hedgerow animal is the hedgehog.

Only 10 inches long and weighing about 2 pounds, hedgehogs are insect eating mammals that use their long, flexible snouts to sniff out food. From spiders, bees, wasps, grasshoppers, centipedes and earthworms to young mice, bird eggs and lizards, hedgehogs feed as they snuffle their way around hedgerows, fields and gardens. Many people place bowls of milk and bread in their gardens to attract hedgehogs to feed on garden pests like slugs and caterpillars.

Hedgehogs are covered with stiff hairs called spines on their backs and shoulders. When a hedgehog is frightened, its skin contracts tightly, causing the spines to stand straight and strong at attention. When a hedgehog curls into a ball, it protects its softly furred belly and vital organs.

Hedgehogs feed heavily at the beginning of autumn because they hibernate through the winter in leaf lined burrows. During the winter their body temperatures fall and their heart rates and breathing drop to conserve energy. When spring comes they wake up hungry. They wander about in search of food. Sometimes they are injured or killed by cars. In Britain, hedgehogs are much-loved animals. In fact, there are hedgehog hospitals across the country to care for the injured hedgehogs.

There are thousands and thousands of miles of hedgerows in Great Britain. Just like the wild habitats of jungles and forests, these man-made habitats must be cared for to protect the animals that make their homes there.

Glossary

▲ *Hedgehog*

▲ *Flycatcher*

▲ *Raspberries*

▲ *Magpie caterpillar*

▲ *Barn owl*

▲ *Hedge garlic*

▲ *Red fox*

▲ *Orangetip butterfly*

▲ *Rabbit*

▲ Draft horse

▲ Primrose

▲ Wood pigeon

▲ Tortoise shell buterfly

▲ Sparrow

▲ Earthworm

▲ Snail

▲ Frog

▲ Heather